God Made You Bouncy, Not Breaky!

Illustrated by Robby Firmansyah
Edited by Missy Bari

Table of Contents

This book is dedicated to Haddie, Eva, Oliver,
Christopher, Norah, Ellis, and Joseph. It is a joy
to train to be bouncy with you!

And to Jemma, it will be such a joy to bounce in the
presence of the Lord with you someday soon!

I love you all,
G

Four Things—That's All!

Bouncy balls are a fun way to play;
they hit the ground but they never stay.

Eggs are yummy scrambled and fried,
but they break when they fall—I know because I've tried!

God made you to be just like a ball: You're "bouncy," not "breaky,"
even when you fall!

Sometimes we feel breaky with no bounce at all,
more like an egg and less like a ball.

When you're feeling breaky like an egg on the floor,
ask others to help you—that's what friends are for!

Feel what you feel (it's important you do), but you can bounce
like balls bounce because that's how God made you!

If you're ready to bounce just like a ball, there are
four things to do; four things and that's all.

Move, move, move, your body needs to move;
to be bouncy not breaky, your body needs to move!

Thank, thank, thank, your thoughts need to thank;
to be bouncy not breaky, your thoughts need to thank!

Love, love, love, give others your love; to be bouncy not breaky,
give others your love!

Pray, pray, pray, your heart needs to pray; to be bouncy
not breaky, your heart needs to pray!

Today is the day to give bouncy a start, so go bounce with your body,
your thoughts, your friends, and your heart!

*Use this QR code to learn a fun
"Bouncy, Not Breaky" song!*

5

Out the Door, Blahsasaur!

Oli was feeling *blah*. Do you know what
blah feels like? I'd guess that you do.

Blah is when you feel sluggish.

Blah makes you want to do nothing.

Your legs feel *blah* because
they don't want to move.

Your mind feels *blah* because
it doesn't want to think.

When you're feeling *blah*,
nothing sounds fun.

Because *blah* makes you feel lazy, and
you just don't care about anything!

Can you picture feeling like that?

Oli was feeling *blah* for one simple
reason: He had let the Blahsasaur
into his room.

What is the Blahsasaur? He's a magical
blue dinosaur with big, sleepy eyes.
He's a smiley, friendly looking creature,
but don't let that fool you—the
Blahsasaur is the one who makes you
feel *blah*. He's the one who makes
you feel like doing nothing.

Why would he do that? It's because he is
kind of lazy and a little bit selfish.
He doesn't like to go outside. In fact,
he doesn't like to move at all. But he also
doesn't want to be alone, so he casts his
blah spell to make sure you won't go
outside and leave him all by himself.

The truth is that the Blahsasaur feels
blah so he wants you to feel *blah* with
him.

Oli's brother, Ellis, came bouncing into the room.

"Let's go outside and play!" Ellis said.

"No," Oli said. "I just want to keep on doing nothing."

"How do you *do* nothing?" Ellis asked. "That doesn't make sense."

"*Blah!*" Oli said. Then he paused, puzzled. He opened his mouth again to tell Ellis to leave him alone, but all that came out was, "Blah, blah, blah!"

Ellis laughed. He thought Oli was teasing him. But Oli wasn't laughing; he was confused.

Why do I keep saying "blah"? Oli wondered.

"I'm going outside!" Ellis said, and out he went.

Now Oli was alone in his room—or so
he thought. The Blahsasaur was
right beside him.

Did I tell you that the Blahsasaur is
mostly invisible, just like his brother the
Complainagator? Who is that, you ask?
Well, that's another story!

You can't typically see the Blahsasaur,
but you can tell he's around whenever you
feel *blah*. And you can tell you feel *blah*
when you want to keep on doing nothing.

The thing about doing nothing is that the
more you do it, the less you like doing it,
but the more you keep doing it.
It's strange, isn't it? That's because
the Blahsasaur is strange, and he makes
us feel strange ourselves.

Still confused, Oli opened his mouth to see what would come out next. He tried to say "blue" (his favorite color), but all that came out was "blah."

Oh no, he thought, *I feel so* blah o*n the inside that all that comes out of me is* blah *on the outside!*

Now he was feeling more *blah* than ever. He sat down on the floor, and the Blahsasaur sat right beside him. The Blahsasaur wasn't happy either, because feeling *blah* isn't fun. But at least the Blahsasaur wasn't alone in his *blah*.

Suddenly, Oli heard a *thump*. Then another *thump*. And yet another *thump*. At first, he didn't want to get up (when you're feeling *blah*, you don't want to move your body). He just wanted to keep on doing nothing.

But he was curious.

The Blahsasaur hates curiosity because it can be stronger than his *blah* magic.

Eventually, Oli got curious enough to stop doing nothing, so he did something! He got up and looked out the window, and he saw Ellis kicking a ball against the house. Over and over and over.

That looks kind of fun, Oli thought.

What if Oli stops feeling blah? the Blahsasaur worried. *What if he stops doing nothing and starts doing something? He might leave me all by myself. I don't want to be lonely!*

The Blahsasaur tried his very best to cast his *blah* spell on Oli again, but it wasn't working. Now that Oli had done something, he wanted to do something else. It turns out that moving your body—even just a little bit—can help you break the Blahsasaur's spell.

Oli put on his shoes and felt
a little less *blah*.

Oh no, the Blahsasaur thought,
*Oli has done two somethings and now
he isn't doing nothing anymore.*

Oli picked up his baseball mitt and
his ball, and he headed out the door.

The Blahsasaur started crying. "Blah, blah, blah!" he blubbered. But then he got up from the floor and walked over to the window.

Wait a minute—now the Blahsasaur was doing something. He'd moved his body too!

The Blahsasaur saw Oli in the yard playing catch with Ellis. *That looks kind of fun*, he thought, and he started feeling a little less *blah*.

Well, what do you know! The Blahsasaur thought doing something looked better than doing nothing.

The Blahsasaur walked to the door and stood there for a minute. He was a little scared. He had never been outside before! All he had ever done was stay inside and do nothing. What would happen to the Blahsasaur if he went out the door and did something?

Believe it or not, the Blahsasaur felt curious. He used to hate that feeling, but now he wanted to see what would happen. So out the door he went!

The Blahsasaur laughed out loud when
the grass tickled his feet—it felt funny.
Hey, he felt funny, not *blah!*

First the Blahsasaur ran, and he felt
tired but good. Feeling tired was much
better than feeling *blah.*

Next he jumped. Then he jumped again.
Then he laughed again. Now he didn't
feel blah at all.

The Blahsasaur felt happy. Feeling happy
was a lot better than feeling *blah!*

He was doing so many somethings that
he wondered why he had ever wanted
to keep on doing nothing.

Suddenly, Oli and Ellis could see
the Blahsasaur! (He isn't invisible when
he's having fun because he's no longer
feeling *blah!*) They watched and laughed
as the Blahsasaur ran and jumped
all over the yard.

The Blahsasaur was having
the best day of his life.

Now, I wish I could tell you that the Blahsasaur never went back to feeling *blah* and that he never cast his *blah* spell on anyone ever again. I wish I could tell you that Oli never felt *blah* again either. But here's the thing: The Blahsasaur always tries to come back and make us feel like doing nothing is better than doing something.

To be clear, there are times when doing nothing is doing something.

Maybe we're tired and it's time to rest. Resting is good; resting is doing something.

Maybe we're just relaxing and doing nothing sounds kind of fun. In that case, doing nothing is doing something.

But we have to be careful that we don't get stuck in the blah. We can't think that doing nothing is always better than doing something. That's just not true, is it?

Here's what Oli learned that day—it's
a trick that works every single time!
Whenever he feels *blah* and wants to keep
on doing nothing, he can just open his
mouth and say out loud, "Out the door,
Blahsasaur!"

Saying those words breaks the spell and,
before you know it, Oli, Ellis, and the
Blahsasaur are all out the door having
a lot of fun!

Now it's your turn to try it. Whenever
you feel that old *blah* feeling—when you
know you should do something but you
want to keep on doing nothing—then do
yourself and the Blahsasaur a favor.
Start moving your body (even just a little
bit). Then open your mouth wide and say
out loud, "Out the door, Blahsasaur!"

Before you know it, you'll be out of your
house having fun doing something.

Oh, and the next time you're outside
having fun and not feeling *blah*, look
very carefully. You might just see the
Blahsasaur jumping and laughing and
having a great day.

He is so happy when you tell him,
"Out the door, Blahsasaur!"

Let's Think!

- Of course, the Blahsasaur isn't real, but he is a fun way to think about something that is really important. We need to move our bodies to be healthy and to feel our best.

- When we feel *blah*, we don't want to do anything. But the longer we do nothing instead of doing something, the more *blah* we feel.

- There are times we feel *blah* because we are sick and need to rest, and there are times we feel *blah* because we are sad about something, like maybe a friend was mean to us at school. It's okay to feel *blah* sometimes, and it is very normal.

- What the Blahsasaur taught us is that sometimes when we feel *blah*, moving our bodies can make us feel much better. God made us so that we feel better, think better, and even treat each other better when we "get out the door"!

- If it's bad weather and you can't go outside, just remember that you can still move your body in the house! Turn on some music and have a dance party, or do some jumping jacks in your living room. Any movement helps fight off the *blahs*.

- It can be super hard to get up and do something when we feel *blah*, but it takes just one small step to get us moving. Before you know it, you'll be saying, "Out the door, Blahsasaur!"

Let's Talk!

1. Why do you think doing nothing can make you feel *blah*?

2. Can you think of a time when you felt *blah* and moving your body made you feel better? What did you do?

3. Why do you think moving your body makes you feel better?

4. What are your five favorite ways to move your body (running, dancing, playing soccer, riding your bike)? If it's cold or rainy, what are some ways you can move your body without going "out the door"?

5. Which one of those things could you do right now? Are you ready to try it? Jump up and yell, "Out the door, Blahsasaur!" Now go have some fun!

See You Later, Complainagator

"I'm bored," Eli said.

"Me too!" Emmy moaned.

"Go outside and play!" their mom
called from the kitchen.

Their replies came quickly:

"It's too hot!"

"There's nothing to do!"

"Eli won't let me play what I want!"

"Emmy is no fun!"

"What's going on with you two?" Mom asked.
"If you don't find something to do, I will find
something for you. And it won't be fun!"

"You always say that! It's not fair,"
Eli whined.

"Nothing is fun," Emmy complained.
"That's why we are bored,"

"That's it, go outside—now!"
Mom demanded.

Those kids are always complaining and never grateful, Mom thought as Eli and Emmy stormed out of the house.

"Maybe I'll just disappear and see how they like it!" she joked to herself.

As she walked by the mirror in the hall, something caught her eye. She thought she saw—no, it couldn't be!

Poof!

Mom disappeared.

POOF

Now, before we catch up with the kids,
I'll let you in on what's going on here.

The whole family is under the spell of the
Complainagator—a sneaky, magical
creature who is *always* hungry.

Here's the thing about the Complainagator:
He's invisible. You can only see him if you
happen to look in a mirror when he's right
behind you.

If you do see him, you will recognize him right
away. The Complainagator may not seem
scary at first. After all, he's only two feet tall,
and he always has a goofy, toothy gator
grin on his face.

In fact, if you *could* see him, you wouldn't
know whether to run or to laugh! But,
I think you would probably laugh.

Even though he seems funny, what the
Complainagator does isn't funny at all. Plus,
his size changes depending on how much you
feed him. He can be very tiny, or he can grow
so tall that he can hardly fit through a door.

How do you feed the Complainagator?

By complaining, of course!

Whenever you start complaining,
the Complainagator suddenly shows up
(but remember, you can't see him because
he's usually invisible).

When you start feeling grouchy and
everything just seems to bug you,
you can be sure he is nearby.

Then suddenly, you are getting mad,
sad, and finally, you just feel bad.

The Complainagator strikes again!

When the old Complainagator casts his spell, we start thinking that complaining will make us feel better. Of course, it never does, but we keep trying anyway. We complain and then we feel worse, so we complain some more. That's a sure sign that the Complainagator is getting bigger.

The Complainagator has another spell too—he makes us think we can't help our complaining. We all know that we don't *have* to complain, but the Complainagator makes it really hard to stop.

He loves to cast his complaining spell on one unsuspecting person. Then, he watches it spread to another, and then another, and pretty soon, he has ruined everyone's day!

When his magic is working extra well and we complain a lot, the Complainagator can make things go *poof!* The good things right in front of us disappear.

That's what happened to Eli and Emmy's mom.

Now that you know this, please don't tell Eli and Emmy. They have to figure this mystery out for themselves or they will never be able to break the Complainagator's spell.

Eli and Emmy were sitting on the porch, feeding the Complainagator some yummy food.

"Don't sit so close! Your leg is touching mine!" Eli yelled.

"You're being a baby," Emmy said.

Emmy knew Eli hated to be called a baby, and she felt a little bad saying it. But Eli had hurt her feelings, so she wanted to hurt him too.

Instead of having fun together on a beautiful day, Eli and Emmy were pouting, complaining, and becoming more and more unhappy.

They couldn't see the Complainagator standing behind them grinning his goofy, toothy gator grin. He was getting bigger and bigger by the minute.

Eli and Emmy were having a terrible day, but that old Complainagator was having a great day!

Eli felt sad, so he decided to ride his bike. He loved his bike. He got it for his birthday last year, and it was blue and really fast. Normally, riding his bike made him feel happy.

But today, the Complainagator's spell made Eli complain about it.

Owen has a better bike than I do, Eli thought. *I hate this bike.*

Feeling grumpy, Eli climbed on his bike. But just as he tried to sit down—*poof!* He fell to the floor. His bike was gone!

"Ouch!" Eli yelled, his bottom hurting a little bit.

Emmy came running. "What happened?"

"My bike just disappeared!" Eli cried.

"See! You *are* a baby! Bikes don't just disappear," Emmy laughed. "Watch this!"

Emmy wanted to convince Eli that she was having a good day, even though she really wasn't. She ran across the yard to kick her favorite ball as hard as she could. *Poof!* went the ball, and *Oof!* went Emmy as she fell to the ground.

At first, Eli and Emmy were just surprised.
Then, they got a little worried.
What was going on?

Without saying a word, they got up and walked
to the backyard so they could swing and think.
Swinging is usually good for thinking,
but Eli and Emmy were so busy complaining
that even swinging didn't help.

The Complainagator was right behind them
and *poof*! The swing set disappeared!

This was really getting strange. Eli and Emmy
ran into the house and yelled at the same time,
"Mom!"

Nothing.

They walked into their parents' room, and
whispered quietly, "Mom?"

Nothing.

Suddenly, the room around them became all blurry, like a wet watercolor painting, and then *poof!* The house was gone, and they were left standing outside.

The Complainagator stood where the house used to be. He wasn't two feet tall anymore. He was now taller than Eli and Emmy but they still couldn't see him

Suddenly, the green grass turned an ugly gray.

(Yep, the Complainagator can even make color disappear!)

Then, the sky turned an ugly gray too, just like the grass.

(Color is such a good thing, but we don't really think about it too much, do we?)

For Eli and Emmy, the world looked just like they felt: very sad.

Now what happened next is really important, so pay close attention.

Eli and Emmy were still sad, but they also started missing their mom and their house and their toys and even the color green.

Why is that important?

Well, the Complainagator's spell started losing some of its power because they had stopped complaining. They still didn't even know the Complainagator existed (let alone how to stop him), but at least nothing else was going *poof!* and disappearing.

In fact, now that they were not complaining anymore, they were able to start working together. They were actually very smart and fun kids when they weren't complaining.

When we complain, we are not being smart or fun. Instead, we miss out on a lot of good things.

It's almost like the good things all around us start disappearing.

"Wait a minute!" Emmy said. "Eli, we have been complaining all day. I wonder if some of this is happening because of that?"

"What? That doesn't make sense," Eli said.

"Well, do disappearing moms, toys, houses, and colors make sense?" Emmy asked.

"No, I guess not," Eli mumbled.

Eli and Emmy became very, very sad. "What if our mom, our house, our toys, and all the colors never come back?" They both cried together.

As they sat in the gray grass where their house used to be, they thought about how their mom would be making them lunch right now. They began to think about how much they loved her. Eli and Emmy were sitting so close that they bumped into each other, and instead of complaining about it, they held each other's hands. It made them feel a little better; they felt happy and grateful.

Eli is a good brother, at least sometimes, Emmy thought.

Eli smiled at her. *Emmy is a kind sister, at least sometimes*, he thought.

The Complainagator was still lurking behind them. *Oh no*, the creature thought. *It's happening.*

Suddenly, the grass started turning green. The Complainagator began to shrink as his complaining magic lost some of its power.

"Eli, I have an idea," Emmy said.
"Tell me some things you are grateful for."

"Well, I can tell you *who* I should have been grateful for, but now she's gone," Eli said, and then he started to cry.

Suddenly, *unpoof*! Mom was standing in front of them.

"Mom!" they both yelled and ran to hug her.

"What's going on?" she asked.
Then she noticed the house was gone.

"Oh, I see," she said.

"See what? You know about things going *poof*?" the kids asked.

"Yes," Mom said. "It happened to my brother and me when we were kids."

She pulled Eli and Emmy in close.

"I wish I could say I learned my lesson, but it's hard to stay grateful when we feel like complaining," she said. "Have you seen any signs of the Complainagator?"

"What? Who?" Eli and Emmy asked.

"Oh, I guess he's still invisible," Mom said. "I saw him in the hallway mirror just before I went *poof!* The Complainagator shows up when he smells a house full of complaining. He loves to eat up all the complaints, and as he eats, he gets bigger and bigger. That's when good things start disappearing."

Eli and Emmy stared at her, their eyes wide and their mouths open.

"Actually," Mom continued, "the good things don't *really* disappear, but you just can't see them anymore. You can never see the good around you when you're complaining. That's why it's so important to fight complaining with its opposite."

"What's the opposite of complaining?" Eli asked.

"Well," Mom said, "we called it *hunting the good stuff!*"

"What does that mean?" Emmy asked.

"One day after we had complained and complained, things started going *poof!* Even my brother went *poof!* right in front of me," Mom remembered. "I was really sad, and I started thinking about all the good things in my life that I missed. Suddenly, *unpoof!* My brother was back! I happened to be standing in the bathroom when, just then, I looked in the mirror and saw the Complainagator behind me."

Emmy gasped.

"Were you scared?" Eli asked.

"He surprised me with his goofy, toothy gator grin!" Mom said. "But then I realized he was shrinking. 'Quick,' I said to my brother. 'Help me hunt the good stuff!' We started listing all the things we were grateful for, and as we did, the Complainagator got smaller and smaller. Eventually, *poof!* the Complainagator disappeared and unpoof! everything good came back!"

Eli and Emmy cheered.

"Let's try it!" the kids said. "Let's hunt the good stuff!"

Eli and Emmy began to shout out all the things they were grateful for. Turns out, there were quite a few of them! All around, things started reappearing.

Unpoof! The green grass was back.

Unpoof! The blue sky was back.

Unpoof! Eli's bike and Emmy's ball were back.

Unpoof! The whole house was back.

Even though they still couldn't see him, the Complainagator, with his goofy, toothy gator grin, was standing behind them. As they listed all the things they were grateful for, he shrank smaller and smaller until *poof!* he was gone.

But was he really gone for good, or was he just waiting for the complaining to come back? What do you think?

Remember, when that old Complainagator shows up and you start feeling mad, sad, and bad, all you need to do is practice being grateful by hunting the good stuff. Then you'll know the Complainagator is shrinking, and you can say:

"See you later, Complainagator!"

Let's Think!

- Of course, the Complainagator isn't real, but he is a fun way to talk about something that is very important. We need to learn how to be grateful!

- Complaining makes us feel mad, sad, and bad because we are not thinking about all the good things God has given us.

- Complaining isn't the same as telling people when you feel mad, sad, scared, or hurt. It's really good to talk to people about those things, isn't it?

- Choosing to stop complaining doesn't mean you don't have things that you don't like or circumstances that are very hard. Everyone has things they wish were different, so it's okay to not always feel happy!

- Complaining doesn't really make things disappear, but it can cause us to forget how many blessings we have. The Complainagator reminds us to be grateful for the good stuff we do have in our lives.

Let's Talk!

1. Why do you think complaining makes you feel mad, sad, and bad?

2. Why do you think it's so hard not to complain sometimes, whether out loud or in our hearts?

3. Why do you think hunting the good stuff helps you feel better? Why is this so important?

4. What can you do the next time you are under the spell of the Complainagator?

5. Grab a family member or a friend, and make a list of the good stuff in your life right now. That way, you'll be ready the next time that old Complainagator shows up!

Please be Kind,
Porcupine!

Chris was annoyed. His little brother, Joseph, kept following him around, and he just wanted to be left alone. Then, Joseph knocked over Chris's Lego tower and that made Chris mad.

Now, Chris is usually a really kind, patient big brother, but today he just felt *prickly.*

Do you know what *prickly* means?

Prickly is when you feel easily annoyed by others. *Prickly* is when you don't feel like being kind or friendly. If others try to get close to you, watch out! You will use unkind words or an unfriendly attitude to make them go away.

Prickly is when you feel more like a porcupine than a person.

Porcupines are *prickly* because they are *stickily!* If you get too close to a porcupine, you'll get stuck by a *prickly stickily* thing. (I think they're called quills.) Ouch! A porcupine uses its *prickly stickily* quills to make sure other animals keep their distance.

We become like porcupines when we do and say unkind things to make others stay away from us.

73

It's okay to want to be alone; we all need time by ourselves. We spend time by ourselves so we can be ready to go have fun with others.

Time alone doesn't make us selfish, but becoming *prickly* does.

What's the difference between needing time alone and becoming *prickly*? Wanting to be alone can be wise and healthy, but when we're *prickly*, we're only thinking about ourselves and not about others.

Chris wanted to get away from his little brother, so he went outside to move his body. That's a good thing. After all, he didn't want to get the *blahs* from that old Blahsasaur. But he didn't know that the Complainagator was standing right behind him.

Chris walked around the yard and thought about all the ways Joseph annoyed him. As he did, the Complainagator ate up all of that yummy complaining, and he grew bigger and bigger.

But the Complainagator wasn't his biggest problem.

Chris's biggest problem was yet to come.

Joseph followed Chris outside.

"Go away!" Chris yelled.

This hurt Joseph's feelings, so he went back inside. Chris felt a little bad and a little sad. But then, *pop! A prickly stickily* quill suddenly popped out of Chris's back.

"Ouch!" Chris said.

Pop, pop, pop! Three more quills popped out of his hands. At first, Chris felt a little scared, but then he had an idea.

Maybe Joseph will leave me alone now, he thought, admiring his quills.

Pop, pop, pop! More quills appeared all over Chris's body. Because Chris felt *prickly*, he had been unkind to Joseph. But after being unkind to Joseph, he felt even *pricklier*.

That's because the unkinder we are to others, the more *prickly* and unhappy we become. And the more *prickly* and unhappy we become, the unkinder we are to others. Do you see how this works? We sometimes think that being selfish will make us feel better, but it always makes us feel worse.

79

You would think that Chris wouldn't want any more quills popping out of his skin (ouch!), but now Chris was thinking more like a porcupine and less like a good big brother.

This is great, Chris thought. *If I'm covered with prickly stickily porcupine quills, then Joseph will never bother me again!*

Suddenly, there were a thousand popping sounds, one after another, and Chris was more of a porcupine than a boy!

Chris walked around the yard enjoying being *prickly*. He picked up his favorite ball and *pop!*

But this time, it wasn't the sound of a new quill. It was the sound of Chris's ball popping because of a *prickly stickily* quill on his hand. That made Chris sad.

Chris went and sat on the swing, but that wasn't fun either because his *prickly stickily* quills hurt his bottom. Being a porcupine wasn't turning out to be as fun as he thought it would be.

He was starting to think less like a porcupine and more like a brother again, but he still looked like a porcupine. What was he going to do with all these *prickly stickily* quills?

Chris went inside to look for Joseph.
He didn't feel like being alone anymore;
he felt like playing with someone else.

When Chris walked into the house, his mom
screamed, "A porcupine!" And out the back
door she ran.

Joseph came downstairs and saw a porcupine, but this porcupine looked a lot like his brother Chris!

"Please, don't run!" Chris said in a loud, scratchy porcupine voice. He started crying *prickly stickily* tears that stuck into the couch and the floor. "I'm not having fun being a *prickly* porcupine. I'm so sorry I was unkind to you, Joseph!"

Joseph picked up a pillow and used it as a shield so that Chris's *prickly stickily* tears wouldn't poke him. He walked over to Chris.

"I forgive you, Chris," Joseph said.

Chris stopped crying. He wasn't feeling as *prickly* anymore. In fact, he wasn't feeling very selfish either. He was feeling love for his brother. He wished he could give him a hug. He wished he could play Legos with Joseph, but he couldn't because he was still a porcupine!

Oh, why had he been so *prickly*?

Suddenly, Chris heard a *pop*!

Oh no, he thought, *I just grew another* prickly stickily *quill.*

But, wait! Instead of a new quill, this *pop* was the sound of a quill disappearing.

Pop, pop, pop! All the quills started disappearing. Before long, Chris wasn't a porcupine anymore. He ran and gave Joseph the biggest hug ever.

"I hope I never become a *prickly* porcupine again!" Chris said.

"Me too," Joseph said with a smile. "But if you do, I know how to fix it."

"You do?" Chris asked. "How?"

"Well," Joseph said, "The next time you start feeling selfish and unkind, all *prickly* and *stickily*, just tell yourself, 'Please be kind, Porcupine!'"

Let's Think!

- Of course, people don't really turn into *prickly* porcupines, but it's a fun way to think about something that is really important. Life is very hard and very sad if we don't have anyone to have fun with. We need each other!

- There are times when we want to be alone, and there is nothing wrong with that! In fact, having some time alone can help you get ready to have fun with others. Needing time alone is fine, but it's never good to be unkind to others.

- When we are feeling *prickly*, we need to learn to tell others how we feel rather than acting in ways that might hurt them. Even if you feel *prickly*, you can choose to be kind. You are not a porcupine; you are a person, and people can choose how they treat each other!

- It can be hard to be kind to others when we feel like a *prickly* porcupine, but Jesus tells us we need to treat each other like we want them to treat us. We don't want others to be *prickly* porcupines with us, do we?

Let's Talk!

1. Why do you think you sometimes feel like a *prickly* porcupine?

2. When you want some time alone, how can you tell others without becoming *prickly* and unkind?

3. How does it make you feel when someone is unkind to you? What about when someone is kind? How can remembering these feelings help you be kind to others?

4. It can sometimes feel good at first to become a porcupine, but after a little while, you start feeling bad. Why do you think this is true?

5. When you feel like a *prickly* porcupine, one of the best things you can do is find ways to serve others. Serving others helps your heart to be soft instead of *prickly*. What are some ways you could be kind to your family and friends that would show them that you love them (draw them a picture, write them a card, ask them to play, help them clean their room)?

One day, Haddie came home from school feeling very sad. Her best friend had ignored her at lunch, so she had to sit with some kids she didn't know. It makes sense that Haddie felt sad, and there's nothing wrong with that. Everyone feels sad from time to time.

But on this particular afternoon, Haddie wasn't just feeling sad. She was feeling *boingy*.

What does it mean to feel *boingy*? It's where you feel one way, then you feel another way, then you feel that first way again. You go *boing* from feeling to feeling to feeling.

Boinging from feeling to feeling can be a problem. For one thing, it's exhausting, and it can make you very unhappy. But *boinging* from feeling to feeling becomes an even bigger problem when instead of just feeling our feelings, we start believing that they are always true.

Feelings aren't all bad; they just aren't all true.

Haddie went from feeling sad because her friend ignored her to feeling like her friend hated her to feeling like nobody at school liked her. She was believing something that wasn't true, and now she never wanted to go to school again!

Haddie's sister, Eva, walked into the room.
Haddie was sitting on the bed with
her head down, looking very sad.

"What's wrong, Haddie?" Eva asked.

Haddie didn't answer her.

"Haddie!" Eva said again, raising her voice.
"You didn't answer me!"

Now Eva was feeling *boingy*. She felt like Haddie
never listened to her (that's not actually true
but she felt it), she felt like Haddie didn't love
her (also not true), and she felt like maybe
there was something wrong with her.

She started believing that everything
she felt was true.

Boing, boing, boing.

Whew, it's so tiring *boinging* from feeling to
feeling. And it's even worse when you start
believing that everything you feel is true.
You'll soon find out why!

Haddie and Eva's cousin Norah heard Eva talking loudly, so she went to find out what was going on. When she got to their room, she froze in the doorway.

Instead of her cousins, there were two kangaroos jumping around. *Boing, boing, boing* they went from here to there and back again.

"Haddie? Eva?" Norah called out.

Where are they? she wondered. *Do they know there are kangaroos in their room?*

The kangaroos stopped *boinging* and looked at her. Now that they'd stopped *boinging*, Norah could see that one kangaroo was orange (Haddie's favorite color) and the other was purple (Eva's favorite).

That's when Norah realized it:
The kangaroos were her cousins!

Her mouth opened wide in surprise.

Just in case you think being a colorful kangaroo and going *boing, boing, boing* sounds fun, please think again.
No one was having any fun at all.

Kangaroo Haddie and Kangaroo Eva were exhausted from all that *boinging*. Plus, they were feeling very sad, lonely, and anxious because their feelings were bossing them around.

Feelings can be good things, but they are not good bosses!

Even though Norah wasn't *boinging*, she was very concerned about her cousins. They were *boinging* so much that she couldn't play with them. In fact, she couldn't even talk to them!

"What happened to you?" Norah asked.

"What do you mean?" Haddie replied angrily.

"Yeah, what are you trying to say?" Eva said with a kangaroo frown on her face.

"What do you mean *what do I mean*?" Norah cried. "You're kangaroos!"

"What of it?" the kangaroos said. "Norah doesn't like us either!"

Norah jumped out of the way as the orange and purple kangaroos *boinged, boinged, boinged* all over the room.

"I don't have any friends, and I never will!" Kangaroo Haddie said as she went *boing*.

"So, what! Even my own family doesn't love me!" Kangaroo Eva said as she went *boing*.

Every time they had a new feeling that made them believe something that wasn't true, they went *boing* again.

Norah was very puzzled. Wouldn't you be?
How could she get her cousins back?
What had turned them into kangaroos
in the first place?

She started paying careful attention to
whenever Kangaroo Haddie and Kangaroo Eva
said anything that made them go *boing*.

"Only bad things happen to me." *Boing*.

"If I don't get an A in math, Dad will be so mad.
Maybe he won't like me anymore." *Boing*.

"Everyone at church is better than I am." *Boing*.

"I wish I looked like Betty. Then I would have
more friends." *Boing*.

Wait a minute, Norah thought. *They're saying things that aren't true. They're believing what they feel but not what is real. Is that what turned them into kangaroos?*

She had to do something, but what could she do? She prayed a prayer for wisdom. She also prayed a prayer for strength, because she was starting to feel like maybe she was wrong and her kangaroo cousins were right. She started thinking maybe she wanted to go *boing* too.

But I can't go boing, Norah realized. *I need to help my cousins. I have to believe what is real, not just what I feel.*

By now, her kangaroo cousins were so tired that they couldn't *boing* anymore. They just sat there looking like two very sad and confused orange and purple kangaroos.

Suddenly, Norah had a great idea! Maybe she could help her cousins remember what was real instead of believing whatever they might feel.

"Haddie? Eva?" Norah said.
"Will you please play with me?"

"But you don't like playing with us,"
Haddie said as she went *boing*.

"Well, then why did I ask you to?" Norah replied.

"Because you are being nice," Eva said.
She didn't go *boing*.

"Maybe you do like playing with us," Haddie
said softly. She didn't go *boing* either.

"I'm being nice because I like playing with you,
and because I do like you,"
Norah said with a smile.

Kangaroo Haddie and Kangaroo Eva started
believing what was real, and as they did, they
turned back into cousin Haddie and cousin Eva.
Norah ran over and gave them both a big hug.

Haddie and Eva were so happy to not be kangaroos anymore that they started running around the room and jumping up and down. *Boing, boing, boing!*

Oh no! Norah thought. *It's happening again.*

"Don't worry!" Haddie said. "We're going *boing* because we believe what is real, not just what we feel!"

"Yeah, and guess what?" Eva said. "That makes us feel like going *boing* right now!"

The next thing you know, Haddie, Eva, and Norah were all going *boing* all over the room, but they didn't turn into kangaroos! They stayed happy cousins, and they had a blast playing together.

In this case, doing what they felt was just fine! Haddie, Eva, and Norah now knew that they could feel what they feel, but still believe what is real.

Remember, feelings aren't all bad; they just aren't all true.

From that day on, if Haddie, Eva, and Norah ever started letting their feelings boss them around, they would jump up and say, "That's not true, Kangaroo!"

Let's Think!

- We can feel a lot of different things, and our feelings are important. But not everything we feel is actually true, is it?

- It is good and helpful to tell your parents or friends what you are feeling, but it's not always good or helpful to believe or to do something just because you feel it.

- What God has said is true even if we don't feel like it is.

- We need to learn how to feel what we feel but to always believe what is real!

Let's Talk!

1. What are some things in the Bible that God says are true? How are these things different from what sometimes feels true?

2. When was a time you felt *boingy*? What were some of the feelings that bossed you around? Did being bossed around by your feelings help you or make things worse? Why do you think this is true?

3. Can you think of a feeling you have had that was okay to believe and okay to do something about? Maybe you felt happy, so you danced. Maybe you felt sad, so you cried. Feelings are not all bad, but they aren't all true.

4. Asking for help in believing what is real and not just what you feel is important. Who can you remember to ask for help when you are feeling *boingy*?

5. What can you do to help you remember to say, "That's not true, Kangaroo!" when you need it? Could you make a sign for your wall with a kangaroo on it? Do you have any other ideas to help you remember?

The Grown-Up Pages:
A Guide to Helping Kids Become More Resilient

These pages are not for kids; they are written to help you understand how you and the children in your life can become more resilient. This section will give you a basic overview of the four pillars of resilience as well as some important concepts that will help you as you help your children, grandchildren, nieces, nephews, students, or any other kids in your care develop their resilience.

I had the great privilege of serving as an Air National Guard chaplain for twenty-six years. I deployed twice; the last time was to Iraq in 2009. The impact of a long war was clearly evident in the lives of military members and their families, and in 2007, the adjutant general of Kansas asked me to help develop a resiliency program for members of the National Guard. The program focused on four pillars of resilience: physical, mental, relational, and spiritual. I was tasked with helping develop the spiritual pillar. In what is now called Comprehensive Airmen Fitness, these four pillars form the foundation of the training.

Over the years, I have used the content contained in these pages to train military members, business leaders, nonprofits, churches, and children in resilience practices. During the COVID-19 pandemic, I was able to field-test resilience practices for children in a real-world crisis. I developed training for our church that was sent out weekly while kids were stuck at home. The feedback from parents regarding a proactive four-pillar focus in their children's lives was overwhelmingly positive.

There is no good model for human thriving that does not include the physical, mental, relational, and spiritual pillars. I pray this book will help you and the children in your life learn to be more "bouncy"!

Bouncy, Not Breaky
A common analogy for resilience is to contrast a ball and an egg. The resilient person is said to bounce like a ball while the non-resilient person is said to break like an egg. But real life is not as simple as being either a ball or an egg. We can all be more "breaky" than "bouncy" at times, there are many factors. Some factors are in our control and

others are not. Even if you tend to be bouncy, it still hurts to hit the ground. Nevertheless, it is a helpful (though imperfect) model for thinking about life and how to grow in our capacity to bounce.

This book is called God Made You Bouncy, Not Breaky! because our kids are resilient. They are born with the capacity to bounce. This doesn't mean that they can't break, but it does mean that we can help them train to bounce more consistently.

Changing Your Mindset

It's important to pause here to make a distinction between training and trying. A trying mindset tends to think in terms of passing or failing, and when we fail—which we will at times—we are prone to quit. A training mindset, on the other hand, helps us understand that success and failure are both a part of growth. When we fail, we don't quit. Instead, we continue to train. This book is a training manual to help our kids develop the reflexes that will allow them to more consistently bounce after encountering events that increase their stress exponentially—what I refer to as one of life's many "bangs."

Everyone will have a bang (actually multiple bangs) in the course of their lives. These might include a health crisis, the loss of a loved one, or multiplied smaller bangs that add up in a cumulative fashion. During these distressing periods of time, most of our energy goes to the crisis at hand, and we are forced to rely on the skills and habits we have previously developed in order to move toward a "new normal." If we have not adequately developed healthy patterns before the bang hits our lives, then we will be less prepared for these stressful times. This lack of preparation can cause the negative effects of the event to last longer and to have a greater impact on our lives. It can also hamper our capacity to move into post-bang growth.

We wish bangs would not come for us or for the children we love, but we all know that they will. Fortunately, we do not have to merely wish for resiliency when we need it. There are things we can do proactively, or "left of the bang," to prepare for endurance during the bang as well as be equipped for growth "right of the bang." There are things we can train our children in that will help prepare them for the hardships they will encounter in life. To train left of the bang means that before the next stressful event comes, we must pay attention to the four pillars of resilience: physical, mental, relational, and spiritual. Then, when the stressors come, this training allows us to navigate through them and continue to thrive and grow right of the bang. Rather than seeing life's bangs as one-time opportunities to either succeed or to fail, we can adopt a training mindset and start building resilience now in order to be better prepared for future obstacles.

Fitness vs. Faithfulness

Another way to think about resilience training is to contrast fitness with faithfulness. Let me illustrate this idea with a story. My friend Jimmy had cerebral palsy from an accident at his birth. He lived in constant pain and with severe physical limitations. Once, he rolled from his bed while he was sleeping and spent the entire night trapped between the bed and the wall. This kind of thing was an ongoing fact of his life. One day I went to see Jimmy at his assisted living complex. As I pulled up, he was standing beside his wheelchair holding on to a flagpole. I got out of my car and walked over to him.

"What are you doing, Jimmy?" I asked.

"Exercising," he replied casually.

To me, it looked like he was standing holding a flagpole, nothing I would consider exercise. Then I noticed the sweat on his brow, and I saw his arms and legs trembling. He was exercising. Jimmy was never going to be what anyone would call physically fit. He was, however, exercising physical faithfulness.

This fitness versus faithfulness contrast applies to all four pillars of resilience. For example, we may not have a "fit" relationship because relationships involve the choices of at least two people. We can, however, be faithful in doing our part to make the relationship thrive. Focusing on fitness alone can potentially mean we're paying too much attention to factors we cannot control. However, focusing on faithfulness means we're paying careful attention to what we can control. Keeping faithfulness as our focus helps us pay attention to our own agency. Knowing we have agency brings hope, and hope inspires action.

Self-Care Is Leadership

As you work with children on resilience training, it will help you grow in your own ability to bounce as well. Whether you are a parent, grandparent, relative, teacher, or caregiver over children in any capacity, you must see self-care as love. If you have flown before, you have likely heard a flight attendant give the speech that instructs you, in the case of an emergency, to put an oxygen mask on yourself before you put one on a child traveling with you. Normally this kind of behavior would sound selfish, but we know that there are times when taking care of ourselves first is not selfish; it is necessary.

Resilience training is one of those things. We must give personal attention to growing in resilience so that we can be equipped to lead and love the children in our lives. Self-care is not selfish; it is leadership. A better word for *self-care* is *self-control*. Self-control is self-leadership. We need to learn to lead ourselves, to not be bossed around by our moods and feelings, in order to grow in our capacity to lead others well. Specifically, we want to be able to lead children well so that they will thrive as they grow into adulthood.

We treasure them, so we train ourselves. We train ourselves so that we can communicate, demonstrate, and celebrate what a resilient life looks like—for the glory of God and good of the next generation.

A Resilient Life Overview

Much like an automobile, which does not run for long without oil, gas, coolant, and air, a human body does not survive for long without food, water, air, and sleep. Likewise, there is no good model for human thriving that doesn't include the physical, mental, relational, and spiritual pillars. We cannot thrive without adequate health and balance in all four of these key areas of life.

> **Physical:** The basics of physical health include adopting and sustaining a balanced diet, regular exercise, and adequate sleep patterns, as well as avoiding negative physical behaviors.
>
> **Mental:** The basics of mental health include adapting and sustaining patterns of thought that are in line with what is true, good, and helpful, as well as avoiding wrong patterns of thought.

Relational: The basics of relational health include building and sustaining honest, enjoyable, and encouraging relationships with people, as well as an awareness and avoidance of negative patterns of relating to others.

Spiritual: The basics of spiritual health include adopting and sustaining beliefs and values that foster a lifestyle of living for something greater than ourselves. The Department of Defense approaches this pillar in a more generic fashion, but as a follower of Christ, I believe spiritual health is described and prescribed in the Bible. The Bible gives the specifics of what leads to spiritual health as well as what undermines it.

These four areas of focus work together in our lives to build and sustain overall health. We can be "low" in one of the four areas and sustain resiliency, but we cannot be "no" in any of the four areas over a long period of time and expect to thrive.

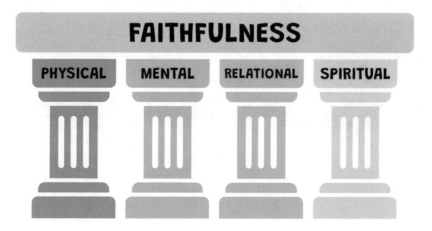

Resilience Training
Left of the Bang

As we talked about, we will all experience multiple bangs, or periods of exponentially increased stress, in our lives, even as much as we wish we wouldn't. During those difficult seasons, we need to be able to fall back on skills and habits that we've already developed to help get us through, and we do that by training left of the bang.

To train left of the bang means that before the next stressful event comes, we must pay attention to the four pillars of resilience—physical, mental, relational, and spiritual. Paying attention includes having a plan, living with accountability, and doing regular self-evaluation. Then, when stress comes, the training we have already done will allow us to navigate through it and continue to thrive and grow right of the bang.

What if you are *already* in the middle of a stressful time and feel unprepared? Even though you can't develop new patterns quickly, you can begin, even during a bang, to work on those four areas of resilience. The best time to work on resiliency is always *right now*!

TRAIN!   PRACTICE!   GROW!

Good Stress and Bad Stress

We all experience stress, but not all stress is bad or harmful. When you are in a challenging situation, your body releases stress hormones. You feel this when you are nervous, afraid, excited, or experience other similar emotions. This heightened mental/physical response is normal, and it can be helpful because it provides extra physical energy and focused mental attention when you really need it. It might help you escape danger, pass a test, give a speech, or accomplish a task at work. The good type of stress is sometimes called *eustress*. (The prefix *eu* means "good" in Greek; for instance, *eulogy* means "good words.")

When stress becomes ongoing and is not dealt with properly, it goes from being *eustress* to *distress*, or from good to bad stress. Ongoing stress can lead to physical disease as well as relational and mental problems. Eustress is normal and can be helpful, while distress can become toxic. Therefore, we need to learn how to keep life's stressors from turning toxic.

The four pillars of resilience are essential in dealing with stress in healthy ways. Again, we cannot keep all stressful events from our lives, but we can learn to become better at handling stress.

Some stressful events can overwhelm our normal coping abilities. When this happens, what we feel is a normal response to an abnormal event. Maybe our skills and habits are not adequate for this new level of stress. It is during these times that we especially need to understand the importance of leaning into the four pillars. Even when we are overwhelmed, we can maintain resilience if we have practiced the four pillars at some level along the way. Remember though, the best time to work on resiliency is *right now*!

DISTRESS

EUSTRESS

Physical Resilience:
Training, Not Just Trying!

In most sports there is an offensive aspect and a defensive one. Offense is when you score and defense is when you try to keep your opponent from scoring. If you only play defense, you are bound to lose the game, but if you do not pay attention to defense, you are also likely to lose.

Similarly, in physical health there is an offensive side (pursuing healthy patterns of behavior) and a defensive side (avoiding unhealthy patterns of behavior). We will look at physical health from these two different perspectives though they are both part of the same objective: balanced physical health.

Playing Offense

The "big four" of proactive physical health are diet, exercise, sleep, and recreation (or fun). These factors work together to form our overall physical well-being. You do not have to strive for perfection in physical health, but rather, the goal is a *settled direction.* This means to consistently choose to take incremental steps toward health in each of the big four areas. Start where you are, make small improvements each day, and over time you will become a more physically resilient person.

We will not discuss specific diet, exercise, sleep, and recreation strategies here, but instead, we'll focus on how they work together to help us be more resilient. What and how we eat, our level of physical activity, the quality and quantity of our sleep, and our ability to enjoy recreation and have fun all directly impact our ability to deal with stress and live a thriving life. For instance, if we eat fatty foods too late in the day, we will likely not sleep well. If we don't sleep well, we are more likely to respond poorly to the challenges we face during the next day. I lost one of my chaplains as an asset in helping a community recover after a devastating tornado because he did not pay adequate attention to his own physical well-being. He became a "casualty" himself, and I had to send him home. I address the impact of the physical pillar in depth in another book, *Grace and Grit: A Faithful Life*.

Again, this is about a settled direction, not a life of perfection. If you start where you are now and make even one small change to your regular routines, you will be moving in the right direction. The way we are wired as humans is that small victories breed more victories, so just a little movement today can lead to large changes over time.

Playing Defense

The things that negatively impact our physical health are often deeply ingrained habits. Things like poor sleep hygiene, lack of exercise, and the excessive use of alcohol. Therefore, we may have difficulty seeing how we can stop doing these things. Again, the key is to start with incremental changes. Most often, changing harmful habits will necessitate enlisting the help of others—resiliency is a team sport!

Trying vs. Training

To try is to succeed or to fail. If I try to hit a ball, then I either succeed or fail. However, if I am training, then both hits and strikes are a part of the growth process. Of course, training includes trying, but in every aspect of your physical life, it is important to take a training, or a continual improvement approach, to resilience.

You can make changes that will positively impact your physical health. It is important that you understand this fact. Believe this is true, because it is true.

Mental Resilience:
Choose Your Thoughts

In our discussion of mental resiliency, we are looking specifically at our thought patterns: what we choose to think about most. We are not looking at mental health as it is commonly thought of (freedom from depression, anxiety, etc.). Mental resiliency, for our purposes, can be summed up like this: "You can't keep birds from flying over your head, but you can keep them from building a nest in your hair." In other words, we can't choose every thought that enters our minds, but we can certainly choose what thought patterns we allow to stay in our minds.

This is very important because the thoughts we allow to stay in our minds are the thoughts we are allowing to shape our lives. There are thoughts that are simply not helpful, and we can think of these thoughts as "stinking thinking." When something stinks, it needs to be discarded. We can learn to recognize and discard thoughts that stink!

Playing Offense

As in the physical realm, we must learn to play both offense and defense in the realm of our thought patterns. Offense is actively choosing the thoughts we will let shape us. It is commonly believed that we can't choose what we think and that thoughts are not that important. But both of these thoughts are not true. They also illustrate how our thoughts impact our lives. For example, if you think you can choose the thoughts that you will allow to stay in your mind and that it is very important to do so, then you will make the choices necessary to become a resilient thinker. However, if you think you cannot choose these thoughts or that they are not that important, then clearly you will not make the choices to become a resilient thinker.

There are a host of right-thinking patterns that are helpful for mental resiliency. These include practicing gratitude, learning to live in the present (versus the past or the future), and giving people grace. There are many, many more, but for our purposes it is important that you realize that there are some healthy and helpful patterns of thought, and it is within your power to focus on these patterns. When you consistently place the right-thinking patterns before your mind, you will shape your overall life direction in powerful ways.

Playing Defense

There are also many wrong patterns of thought that can adversely impact our mental health (and physical, relational, and spiritual—it all works together). These include what is called the negative bias, which means giving disproportionate weight to the negative versus positive factors in our lives. The important thing to remember is that you can choose not to allow wrong thoughts to nest in your mind. You can practice defending against them.

Relational Resilience:
Live in the Right Column

Picture a blank piece of paper with a line down the middle. In the left column, list all the things that are important or of concern to you but that you do not have control over. In the right column, list all the things that are important or of concern to you that you do have control over. Then, focus your attention and efforts on the right column. This is what it looks like to train for relational resilience.

We all know that some people are more extroverted and others are more introverted. Which are you? Did you know that both extroverts and introverts need a strong, healthy relational network? All human beings need good relationships in order to be fully healthy and to thrive through times of crisis and beyond. Relational health, like other aspects of overall health, is tied to certain attitudes as well as actions.

Attitudes

The attitudes of relational health begin with realizing that it is my responsibility, not someone else's, to build and sustain good relationships. Very often we will wait for others to pursue us and to invite us into their lives. We will also wait for others to initiate forgiveness when the relationship has been damaged. We wrongly assume that someone else should be doing the bulk of the work to build relationships with us. When it comes to pursuing healthy relationships, it's important to cultivate an attitude of ownership. Each person is responsible for themselves.

The second most important attitude is that we must give people grace and let go of unrealistic expectations. It is possible to have good relationships with people, but it is not possible for those relationships to be perfect. Everyone struggles with various insecurities and wrong thought. "They" are not responsible for your personal health and satisfaction—you are! Understand this fact and act on it.

Actions

The actions of relational health start with a very basic idea: show up. By "show up," I mean just start getting time with people. Showing up means that we take responsibility to be there in relationships. It could mean inviting people into our homes, our lives, and our events, as well as showing up for their lives and events. It could mean taking action to forgive or to ask for forgiveness. We don't have to be a perfect match to have a good relationship with someone. Oftentimes the most beneficial relationships are with people who are not just like us. When we show up, "great" things may not always happen, but they can. If we don't show up, we are guaranteed that great things won't happen.

It is important that we realize that just as there are negative physical and mental practices, not all relationships are healthy. Some relationships can adversely impact resiliency. Even though we shouldn't look for perfection in others, it is important that we look for people who have beliefs, values, and behaviors that are generally healthy and positive. We may have family members or old friends who are not positive influences on us, but perhaps we feel we cannot leave these relationships. Nevertheless, it's important for us to also pursue healthy relationships that will help us become more resilient people. To have these kinds of relationships, we must look to be helpful to others—not merely to be helped by them. We should try to be the kind of friend that we would like others to be to us.

Spiritual Resilience:
The Big *Why*

The critical question for the resilient life is, "Do I have to wait until the end of my life to know what matters the most?" Fortunately, the answer is no. You don't have to wait, because what matters the most at the end matters the most now.

What will matter the most at the end will be relationships—relationships with God and relationships with those God has given us to love. Relational resiliency is about building those important relationships with others, and spiritual resiliency is about building our relationship with God.

All Live by Faith

All people live by faith, but it is not how much faith we have that is most important; it is whether our faith is well-placed that matters the most. If you have a lot of faith in a weak bridge, you will fall. However, a little faith in a strong bridge will keep you safe. We want to ensure that our faith is both strong and well-placed.

Spiritual resilience is about living with the big picture in mind. It is living for something greater than yourself and for some time greater than right now. We are created for purposes that are greater than just living day to day like animals. We are created on purpose and for eternity. Though this is true based on reason, experience, and from what God has revealed, it is something that is easily forgotten or neglected. Spiritual health, like all forms of health, takes time and attention. It will not just happen automatically. Spiritual resilience includes paying attention to both our beliefs and our behaviors.

Beliefs

The starting point for spiritual health is to grow in our understanding of what is true about God, us, our purpose, what makes "the good life," and what happens when we die. Spiritual resilience requires that we do the good work to ensure that our beliefs are well-founded and not merely something we have assumed to be true or adopted from someone else. This is important. Life's bangs will test our beliefs, so we want to be sure that our beliefs are both thoroughly examined and put into regular practice.

Behavior

Our behavior is where what we believe turns into what we do. The practice of our faith shapes our lives in tangible ways. Sometimes the word *religion* has negative connotations, and while this is understandable, it is also unfortunate. *Religion* is, in its essence, the practice of faith, and the practices of faith are the very things that build spiritual resilience. These practices include actions like prayer, reading the Bible, worship, serving, and fellowship with others who are trying to grow in relationship with God.

Resilience does not work as an end in and of itself. Rather, resilience is the *how* to be faithful in the bigger *why* of our lives. It all works together!

Pursue a Life of Long-Term Direction

So, what would you prefer to survive without over the long term: air, food, water, or sleep? We can go longer without sleep than air, and longer without food than water, but all are necessary to survive. We cannot choose to eliminate one. We must have all four.

These four physical requirements demand that we pay attention to them. If we are low on air, food, water, or sleep, our bodies will push us to acquire those things in order to survive. When we are low on physical, mental, relational, or spiritual requirements for health, we don't feel the same sense of urgency, but the necessity is there nonetheless.

Perhaps you have ignored your physical health because you have not deemed it as important as other things in your life. It is likely that, over time, without adequate rest or because of a poor diet, you have seen your attitude suffer. In other words, your physical health has impacted your mental health. Then, as the result of those two factors, you have seen your relational health impacted as well. Spiritual health is the most often overlooked component, but without an eternal perspective, we soon lose sight of what really matters, and all of life moves into imbalance.

Remember, this is about direction, not perfection. Please do not become overwhelmed thinking of all the things you have to quickly change or fix in your life. Start with one thing in each area and move forward, one step at a time. If you fail, recover quickly and get back on the path. As you train yourself to continue growing in resilience, you'll be able to better help the kids in your life do the same. A settled direction, not perfection, is the key to the resilient life.

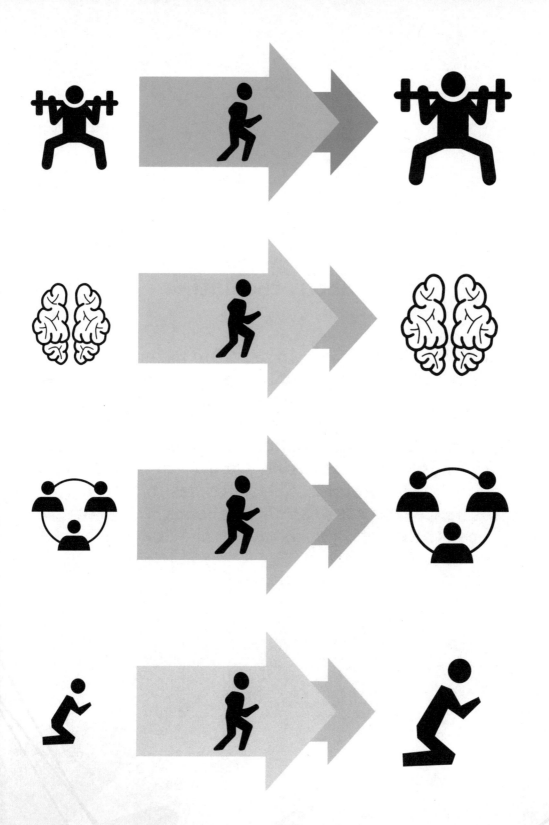

135

About the Author

Dr. Terry Williams, known as "G" to his grandchildren, is a retired Air Force Chaplain and has been a pastor for more than thirty-five years. Terry has developed resilience training programs and materials for the military, businesses, nonprofits, and children, and his work has been field-tested everywhere from combat zones to playgrounds. When it comes to teaching resilience, Terry is passionate about the practical, because the best plan is always the one you will actually do.

Made in the USA
Columbia, SC
11 December 2024

48991679R00076